The Inventions of God (and Eva)

Copyright © 2021 by Dave Connis
Illustrations copyright © 2021 by Andrea Michelle Domingo

Published in the United States by WaterBrook, an imprint of Random House,
a division of Penguin Random House LLC.

WATERBROOK® and its deer colophon are registered trademarks of
Penguin Random House LLC.

ISBN 978-0-593-23355-9
Ebook ISBN 978-0-593-23356-6

The Library of Congress catalog record is available at
https://lccn.loc.gov/2021010748.

Printed in China

waterbrookmultnomah.com

10 9 8 7 6 5 4 3 2 1

First Edition

Book and cover design by Andrea Michelle Domingo
Cover illustrations by Andrea Michelle Domingo

SPECIAL SALES Most WaterBrook books are available at special quantity discounts
when purchased in bulk by corporations, organizations, and special-interest groups.
Custom imprinting or excerpting can also be done to fit special needs. For information,
please email specialmarketscms@penguinrandomhouse.com.

THE INVENTIONS OF GOD

(AND EVA)

STORY BY
DAVE CONNIS

ART BY
AMY DOMINGO

WATERBROOK

This is Eva.

HI!

This is **GOD.**

Kinda.

He's hard to draw.

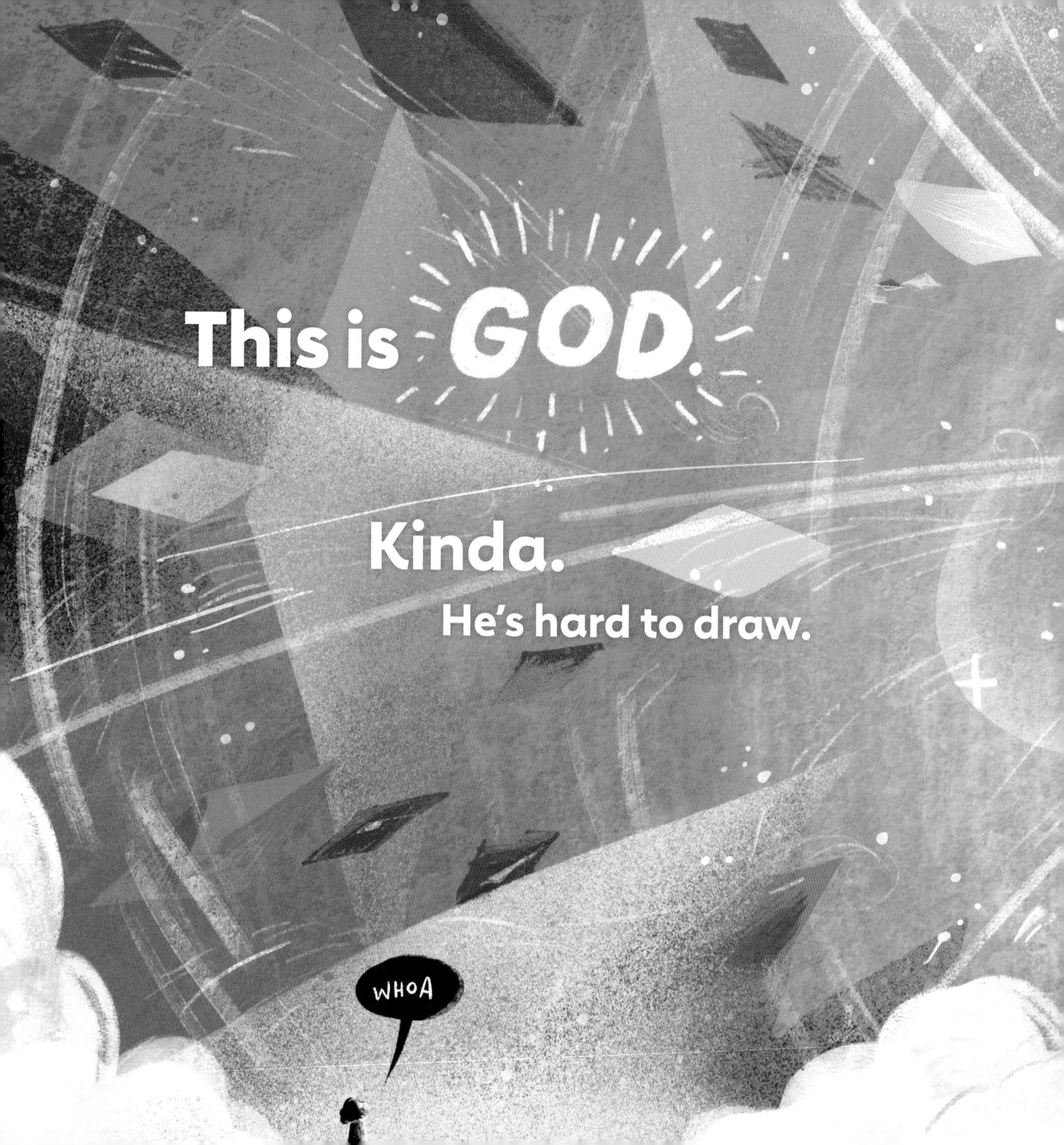

God and Eva are a lot alike . . .

because God made Eva to be just like Him.

Eva and Dr. Michelle Wimbledon Katsworth
the Tenth are also

A LOT ALIKE...

because Eva made
Dr. Katsworth to be

JUST LIKE HER!

God and Eva both love to

INVENT.

This is His

EARTH.

This is His
PLATYPUS.

This is her
LOOFAPUS.

This is His Eva.

This is her Mr. Robotreestuff.

Errr . . . three.

And a half.

Sometimes, God and Eva are different.

For example, Eva thinks the early versions of her inventions lack dazzle, oomph, and maybe pizzazz.

But God thinks everything He makes has tons of dazzle, oomph, and definitely pizzazz.

God invented Eva because He wanted to share the things that make Him happy—things like

inventing,

fixing,

jumping in puddles,

and loving others.

Eva created Mr. Robotreestuff (version 4) because she wanted to share the things that make her happy—things like

speaking fluent robot, organizing nuts and bolts, and serving other people robot tea.

God thinks Eva is  AWESOME.
He loves when Eva does Eva things.

And because God thinks you're

AWESOME, He loves when
you do you things.

God loves being with Eva and talking human.

Eva loves hanging out with Mr. Robotreestuff (version 4.5) and talking robot.

But the thing Eva loves most is taking something broken and making it new.

And since God and Eva are a lot alike,

God loves that the most too.

To Emmie, both God and I love when you do you things.

—DC

To God, thank You for putting all the pieces together to make this book happen! And to Ma, Pa, and Migs, thank you for your love and never-ending support!

—AD